I0518202

THE LAST VERDICT

JAMIE ARPIN-RICCI

ARPIN-RICCI BOOKS

CONTENTS

SUBSCRIBE

For news, updates, and special deal on books by Jamie
Arpin-Ricci, be sure to subscribe at:
www.jamiearpinricci.com/subscribe

PART I
ALICE

Chapter 1

hat does one wear to an execution?

The very thought of asking this question out loud turns my stomach, a sour taste filling my mouth. How else could it be heard other than as a flippant and callous concern in the face of such a serious situation? As I try to imagine actually asking someone this question, I shudder at the thought of what they might say, at the look that most certainly would show on their faces. It matters not one bit that I am genuinely unsure of what is appropriate to wear, that I want to avoid the very disregard that would be assumed in my question. That fact is that it would be heard as an expression of indifference that I most certainly do not feel. I am in no way indifferent to what I will witness today. Long-delayed justice will be exacted on the monster who murdered my only daughter and I will be there because she is not. It's all that is left for me to do for Madeline, though she deserves so much more.

This is why choosing what to wear today is so important, why I wish I had someone to ask—someone who would understand. Someone who would sympathize with my need to look mournful, but not defeated; vindicated, but not vengeful. Byron, of course, would have understood. In fact, I have little doubt that he would have chosen the perfectly appropriate outfit, laying it out for me on our bed without a word while I was in the shower, then slipping off to his study before I emerged. He had a way of doing that—a way of getting things done and meeting our needs without ever being noticed doing so. We'd turn around to find some small kindness done for us, yet no sign of Byron anywhere. Invariably, we would find him in his study, a newspaper folded neatly on his lap as he stared down at a crossword, brow furrowed and pencil poised. He loved that study, which was meant to serve as his home office, but became his sanctuary from the busyness of life. If I could help it, I wouldn't disturb him while he was there unless absolutely necessary. Even the kids learned to respect that sacrosanct boundary without question.

Except for Madeline, of course, who was always Byron's exception- his exceptional girl. Somehow, she could skip through the door, hop onto her daddy's lap and insert herself as the center of his universe in a way her brothers would never have even tried. Byron would smile, lay his folded newspaper aside, and wrap his arms around his little Maddy. Even as a teenager, this ritual continued. Sometimes, not a word would be passed between them. Not even the inevitable turbulence of adolescence could disrupt this almost daily ritual. While he never favored any one of his children more than the others, there is a special bond between a father and his daughter. And so the study became their shared place.

After the murder, Byron began to retreat into the study

with increasing frequency, closing himself in for hours at a time. Sure, as he left for work each day, he would kiss my cheek and pat the boys roughly on their backs, but even then he was not fully present. When his participation in family activities or at the boy's school events began to wane, I became concerned, urging him to stay connected. He tried, I'll grant him that, but no amount of coaxing seemed to work. I'm ashamed to admit that I even tried guilting him into engaging, reminding him that he still had three living children who needed him. This only served to drive him away further. And so we learned to let him be and appreciate those rare moments he emerged from his study to be with us.

Maddy's death had devastated all of us. While Adam, our eldest son, stepped up as best he could, his brothers were traumatized. Michael looked to Adam for support and, in time, worked through the grief. Our youngest, Trevor, already struggling with school, pulled away from the family completely. Yet, it was still Byron who seemed to suffer the worst of it all. The endless days in court seemed to suck the life out of him, and on the nights following the worst of them, he would stay in his study late into the night, tiptoeing back into our room as quietly as he could. As he crawled into bed beside me, I would try to comfort him, wrapping my arms around him. And then he would weep. His body curling in on itself, he wept tears of anger, frustration, and grief. Yet I knew that he wept mostly out of shame—shame for having failed to protect his family from all that had happened; shame for not being strong enough in the midst of the trials; shame for not being able to protect his precious Maddy in the first place.

It was hard on me too, of course, but I had to be the

pillar. I had to be the one who was strong enough to keep us together. No matter how desperate matters felt, falling apart was never an option I could accept. As a wife and the mother of four children... *three* children, withdrawing or giving up was unthinkable. And so I remained steadfast, engaging with the lawyers, the press, the constant flow of people who wanted to show their support, even those who inserted themselves into our lives out of morbid curiosity, vultures seeking to take for themselves any small bit of the spotlight that had been fixed upon our family. Even then, I was the picture of strength, of gratitude, and of resolute purpose. Looking back, I know that I paid too high a price for that false strength. Perhaps today would mark an end to the pretense.

Byron died of a heart attack three months before the judge delivered the sentence. I found him on the floor of his study, collapsed at the foot of his chair. Before that moment, I would have said it impossible to suffer any more grief or pain. I would have said that I had nothing left to give, emptied by the endless and merciless trauma of what we had gone through since Maddy's murder. In that moment, as I threw myself to the ground beside my husband, shaking him by the shoulders in a desperate plea for life, I discovered how wrong I was. The boys later told me that when they found me, I was cradling their father in my arms, rocking back and forth, crying again and again, "Please don't leave me! Please don't leave me!"

Mark Allen Williams was sentenced to death by lethal injection for the murder of our innocent young daughter, Madeline Angela Goodman. The precise and calculated words of the sentence lacked the gravity of what this moment meant. It had taken so long to arrive at that judgment. Perhaps it was for the best that Byron was not there to witness it. Naïvely, I had assumed that this would mark a kind of end to our suffering. And yet, it had been eighteen years since the sentence was handed down—*eighteen years!*—twenty years since Maddy was found murdered. Even as I think of it in this moment, my blood begins to boil as I think about it. For twenty years this killer has been allowed to live and breathe while my sweet girl will never draw breath again. She will never have a chance to pursue her dreams, to find true love, to become a mother. All of that was forever stolen from her, yet this monster lives on. For twenty years *his* family has been able to see him, visit him, talk to him, even hold onto hope as they fight to see his sentence commuted. No, Byron could not have handled this miscarriage of justice. Today, at least, that will finally be put to an end.

Wiping the tears from my eyes, I settle on a modest outfit from the closet—the colors appropriately muted and subdued—and quickly get dressed. This home is filled with the ghosts of these memories, which makes me that much more aware of how completely silent it is. Of course, the boys have long since grown up and moved out. They urged me to sell the house, to get a fresh start and try to leave some of those horrific memories behind, but I refused. I could not run away from the bad memories without also leaving behind the countless good ones as well. This is the home that Byron and I had built together, where we had made a life together, and where we had raised our children. I have lost too much already. I will not let that man take anything else from me. I just wish I was not so tired. So very tired.

Steeling my resolve once again, I refuse to let fatigue win the battle this morning. Anticipating this, last night I had wisely set the coffee maker to automatically brew first thing in the morning, so I make my way to the kitchen. However, as I walk into the room, the now fading aroma of once fresh coffee tells me that I have spent more time getting ready than I had thought. The heating element has long since turned off, and the small pot is already tepid. Glancing at the clock, it is clear that a fresh pot is out of the question. Always punctual, Adam will be here very shortly to pick me up. I remind myself that he will have little patience for my typical tardiness, especially on a day like today where his nerves will be as raw as my own. Of course, always the good son, he wouldn't say anything, but his nervous pacing and frequent peeks at his watch would be telling enough. Pouring the lukewarm coffee into a mug, I decide I will have to make do with warming it up in the microwave.

As the microwave whirs, I carry the pot to the sink and pour the rest of the coffee slowly down the drain. As I do so, I stare out the window overlooking the backyard, a spacious oasis filled with a lifetime of memories. At the edge of our lot, a large wooden fence with a simple latched gate separates the yard from the dark trees of the nature reserve around which our development was built. As a newly married couple just getting started, that added a bit of luxury had cost Byron and me a pretty penny, but it was too beautiful to pass up. It no longer holds the same warm memories for me. I remember standing in this very spot on the night that Maddy went missing, watching the narrow path that broke from the tree line, waiting to see her emerge on her way home, as she had countless times before. Yet, as the shadows of dusk crawled across the familiar landscape, fear had begun to creep into my heart as the darkness swallowed the day.

It was an unusual fear- no different than what every

parent feels more than once as their children grow up and go out into the world on their own more and more. Yet, despite knowing this, my chest had tightened as imagined all the terrible things that might have caused her to be late. No, I would not fall prey to the wild assumptions that I used to mock my own mother for having! Instead, I shifted to anger. After all, it was far more likely that she was out with friends, carelessly unmindful of the time or what it might be doing to those of us waiting at home. I could even imagine her basking in the thrill of defying her curfew. Byron had just smiled at my concern, reminding me that such a small act of rebellion was a rite of passage, far more innocuous than others she might have chosen. She would be home soon enough.

Byron had a way of assuming the best about everyone, especially Maddy. While he might have assumed she was out with her *girlfriends*, I suspected that she was out with that Williams boy again, despite our having forbidden her from seeing him. There was enough talk around town that he was bad news. You could tell just by looking at him. However, too much like her father, Maddy also only saw the best in others, believing that she could save anyone, even from themselves. I had hoped she would have learned her lesson when she had tried to help her younger brother, Trevor, whom she discovered was struggling in school and making some bad choices. Rather than come to us, she had tried to help him. It had not gone well and the tension between the two of them was palpable. Despite her good intentions, she had made things worse. I worried that she would make the same mistake with this *Mark* fellow, letting those same intentions cloud her better judgment. If I found out she was with him, she would be *so* grounded!

By the time the sun had begun to rise the next morning, the heat of my anger had turned into a cold panic. Despite calling every one of Maddy's friends and classmates that we could reach, no one had seen or heard from her since the night before. One of her closest girlfriends reluctantly admitted that Maddy had confided in her that she would be going out with Mark Williams that evening, confirming my earlier suspicion. It became clear that she had been spending a lot of time with Mark, even hanging out at his family's apartment, despite her promise that she would not see him again. Furious, I hunted down a phone number and called him immediately. After his mother put him on the phone, he admitted to having been with Maddy until late the previous night. He was the last person to see her, yet he couldn't—or *wouldn't*—tell us anything helpful at all.

Up until that moment, we had been hoping against all odds that we would find her, with the whole thing amounting to typical teenage drama. Clearly something far more serious was going on, and so Byron called the police. In a frustrating waste of time, the officers who came to the house had spent what seemed like hours asking us endless questions about Maddy's recent behavior, about our relationship with her: Had we had any fights with her lately? Wass there any reason she might want to run away? How were her grades in school? Answering every one of their questions, we pleaded with them to get out there and find her. They assured us, with infuriating calm, that they were doing everything they could possibly do at this point. Finally, after running the gauntlet of procedure, search parties were organized and sent out to look for her. I insisted on joining the search, but the police assured us that it would be better if we were to stay at home, in case Maddy called or returned to the house. "That's usually how these things get resolved, ma'am," said one officer, trying his best to put me at ease.

And so, as the sun set on yet another day when my daughter hadn't come home, I stood again at the kitchen window. Through the branches of the forest, I watched as the beams of dozens of flashlights swept methodically from left to right, moving slowly into the darkness away from the house. Wanting nothing more than for my daughter to be found, I was terrified that one of those beams would, indeed, find her. And, as though reading my very fears, I watched as suddenly all of those lights turned as one and begin rushing to the same distant, unseen spot. It was in that moment that I knew: They had found my Maddy.

The sound of my front door closing mercifully snaps me back to the present. "Mom? You ready?" Adam's voice echoes from the hallway, having let himself in with the spare key. Lost again in memories that I'd rather forget, I had lost track of time and missed hearing him pull up. He peeks his head around the corner, spots me and smiles warmly. Dressed in a tidy yet modest navy suit, he is the image of his father, down to the grey at his temples and the slightly weathered face. For a brief moment, a pang of grief flits through my heart as I am reminded of Byron, wishing he were here with me now. Yet, I am deeply grateful for Adam. He is here for me today like has been there for me and his brothers so many times over the years since Byron's death. He is a good son.

Forced to grow up far too quickly, Adam had needed to give up more than any kid should have to in order to help our family move forward after losing Byron. While never trying to replace Byron, he had become the closest thing to a father his brothers would have from that point on. Now a father himself, he takes care of his own growing family with the same unwavering devotion. A beautiful wife whom he adores, two boys that are the light of his life (and mine, as well), and a solid career that provides for his family without consuming all of his time. In fact, I know that he could have advanced much further in his job, but his refusal to put his family second to his work slowed his ascent. He doesn't regret it in the least, and I couldn't be more proud of him. Smiling at him in welcome, I swallow back the swell of emotions that are hovering just at the edge of my control.

"Come on in, sweetheart. Right on time, as usual. Have you heard from your brothers?" "Michael will be in later this evening," he replies, his smile shifting to a tight frown as steps into the kitchen, "He said he would meet up with us at my place after we're back from the prison. We both know that he could have come earlier, could've been here for today. I have half a mind to—" "Adam," I interrupt him, firmly but gently, "leave it be. You know your brother doesn't want to see the execution. He's been clear on that from the very beginning. That's his decision to make, so we're going to respect that. It's probably for the best anyway. He's always had such a tender heart." "A tender heart? More like a bleeding heart. It's that university he went to up north. Filled his head with nonsense," Seeing the look of reproof on my face, Adam decides to let it drop.

"Have you heard from Trevor?" I do my best to sound casual as I ask this, trying to mask the painful desperation behind my question, but Adam's downcast eyes betray my failure. I know the answer before he responds. In truth, I knew the answer before I had asked the question.

"Mom, you know he's been going through a rough patch again. He called Michael a few months ago, talked about going into rehab again. That fell apart when things started heating up with the case again when this execution date was set. He's never forgiven himself for not making up with Maddy before she died." We both stand there in silence for a moment. "We're not going to hear from him for a while, I'm sure. And most certainly not today. I promise, Mom, I will take a trip out there to check on him when I can get some time off work. We'll get him through this."

Nodding, I look again out the window at the forest beyond the fence. Those woods, where so much had been taken, where so much had ended. While they were where Maddy's life had ended, in a way it was also where Byron's had ended as well. And now, it seemed, they might claim Trevor too. No matter how hard I tried, I could not fight back the devastation the murder had inflicted on my family, that it continued to inflict. Again and again, the inexorable ripples of that unspeakable crime seemed to grow with time, turning into wave upon wave of suffering that poisoned everything it touched. Again, we stand in silence, lost in the darkness of our thoughts.

"I think it's time to get going." Adam clears his throat nervously, glancing at his watch. He has never been comfortable with long silences, one way in which he is very much unlike his father. "Have you had anything to eat?" I smile at his pragmatism, the efficient way in which he shows his love.

"Don't you worry about me. I'm a grown woman. Just come over here and give me a hug." Pulling him into an embrace, his body relaxes slightly. I hold him tightly, almost afraid to let him go, to lose him like I've lost so much else.

"I love you, ma," he says gently, patting my back in his way. "Now, have you eaten anything this morning?" Knowing that I won't survive the day on hugs alone, Adam is not going to let me off the hook. Correctly reading the expression on my face, he jerks his head toward the front door. "I didn't think so. No need to worry, I planned ahead. I picked up coffee and muffins on the way over. You can eat in the van."

I smile at the clutter of toys and tissue boxes in Adam's minivan as he hastily sweeps aside the mess so that I can I climb into the passenger seat. My two grandsons are at home with their mother, Erica. While Adam firmly believed that his brothers should be with us today, he resolutely insisted that his wife not witness the execution, despite her willingness to be there for him, for me. I had agreed with Adam and she had relented, with no small amount of relief, I imagine. I don't blame her. What mother wants to be reminded of such a horrible crime, to witness the cost of such an act, especially when her own children are so young and vulnerable? Better that she stay home with my grandbabies. I smile at the very thought of them, a welcomed, if fleeting distraction from the fore-boding I feel about the day ahead.

"We're meeting at the sheriff's office, then they'll drive us the rest of the way in the prison van. Are you ready to head there now?" Adam asks, buckling his seat belt.

"No, not yet. We have a little time. I want to visit your sister before we go."

Chapter 2

A tomb now suffices him for whom the whole world was not sufficient.

These words, the epitaph of some long forgotten hero, come unbidden into my mind as I walk across the manicured lawn of the cemetery. No matter how expensive the headstone, no matter how beautiful the location, no place could ever adequately honour the life of the child that I lost—the life that she was robbed of too early. In the face of a tragedy such as this, any attempt to do so seems grievously deficient. And yet, we had chosen the most beautiful headstone that we could afford, under a huge oak tree at the top of a small hill. How could we do any less?

Reaching into my purse, I pull out a small, folded handkerchief that I had brought for this purpose, laying it carefully on the thick grass beside Maddy's burial site. Kneeling isn't as easy as for me as it once was, especially not in these formal clothes, but I manage to get down without collapsing. I look sideways at the gravestone, with a crooked grin.

"Don't you laugh at your old mother, young lady. My body may not be as obedient as it once was, but I still got some fight left in me." I immediately begin my ritual of weeding the small plot of grass that blankets my girl. It's unnecessary, for the most part, as they keep the cemetery immaculately groomed. But a mother needs to do something for her child. "You got that from me, Maddy. You were always such a fighter, never backing down from anything, even if sometimes you might have been better off if you had. Do you remember the time you gave Adam a shiner for teasing you about your ears? You were eight years old, for Pete's sake! I was furious, but your father—bless his heart—just smiled, proud as, well, punch. He said he would deal with you while I looked after your brother. If I remember correctly, he ended up taking you out for ice cream.

"Adam's here, by the way, but I made him wait in the van. He comes to visit you regularly, bringing your nephews along with him. I thought it was morbid, taking such little ones to a graveyard, but he thinks it's important. He tells them stories about you with such affection that the kids talk about you as though they knew you, though I'm not sure if they've heard the black eye story yet. Your big brother is a good daddy and you'd like his wife too, I think. She loves Adam very much and loves their kids. I know that you would be very proud of them all.

"Michael's not here yet. He's not coming until later this evening. He didn't want to come to the prison today. He's been respectful about it, but I know he disapproves of our going. I was livid when he first told me that he didn't believe in the death penalty, felt as though he was betraying us—betraying you! Who better than our family knows how necessary proper justice truly is? A life for a life—even the Bible says so. That man needs to get what he deserves. I didn't speak to Michael for a week. He tried to call, of course, but I would have none of it. It was only when I thought about what your father would say that I relented. So, we don't talk about *that* anymore, but we have chosen to love each other in spite of it all. What else can we do? Family is family, after all.

"Trevor still isn't doing too well. He's taken all of this very poorly. I know he was messing around with drugs before you were killed, but losing you seemed to push him over the edge. I suppose that's what the two of you were fighting about. When you died before he could make things right... I'm sure that's been tearing him up inside. I understand, but to pump his own body full of that poison? What could he be thinking? I raised him to know better than that!" I fall silent for a moment. "He doesn't call me anymore. I've not seen him in months. He won't talk to Adam either, though that isn't too surprising. Adam's become something of a father bear since you left us and comes off a bit strong at times, which rubs Trevor the wrong way. I'm grateful that he seems willing to talk to Michael, at least. A small comfort, I guess. I'll say this for Michael: aside from his questionable political persuasions, he has been a safe place for Trevor to land, his only point of connection to the family, really. He got him into treatment once, so let's just hope he can do it again."

I sigh heavily, leaning back on my heels. So much grief, so much sadness.

"I can't help but wonder what you would think about what is going to happen today. After you were... after you died, I was convinced that you would want us—no, *need us*

—to exact some semblance of retribution for what *he* did to you. It was as though your blood was crying out for it. After all, I know you would not want the killer to be free to hurt anyone else. So we fought for you! We fought for the strongest penalty such a crime could receive under the law. It's what you would have wanted. Isn't it? I have to believe that you would, that you do. You have always been such a fighter and you would have wanted us to fight for you!

"Damn it, Maddy, why didn't *you* fight? Why did you let him *do that* to you without tearing the flesh from his bones? They told me that when that boy was brought in for questioning, he didn't have a scratch or bruise on him. How is that possible? How could you let him..." A sob bursts from my throat as I fall forward, my hands on the cool grass and earth of the grave. How could a grief so old still hurt so very much? Yet, time and again, over the years I have returned to this place, demanding the same answers from my daughter and receiving the same stubborn silence. And, like so many times before, the guilt immediately takes hold.

"Oh, sweetheart... I'm sorry. I know it wasn't your fault; none of this is. You may have been a fighter, but you were also the kindest and trusting person I have ever known. Maybe if I had been more firm with you, none of this would have happened. We told you to stay away from that boy, that he would lead to nothing but heartache. But no, you were not to be dissuaded. You saw a wounded soul and you weren't going to turn him away. You were going to change him. You gave your all for him in hope that it would make a difference, and he repaid your kindness by taking everything from you.

"I guess your father and I should have known better. It's not as though we listened to our own parents' warnings when we were your age. If anything, it made us all the more want to go after the very things they warned us about. And so, I failed you there too, I suppose. Yet never in my worst nightmares did I think it would come to this. When you started seeing Mark, I worried he might get you to start drinking, or at the worst to smoke pot. When I caught him kissing you behind the back fence, I was terrified that he'd seduce you and get you pregnant. I never thought he would... Never *that*! Somehow we should have known, should have stopped you. How could *you* have known if *we* didn't even see it?"

Dabbing at the tears welling up in my eyes, I slowly pull myself to my feet, weighed down by the tiredness of both age and grief. Wiping my hands together, I watch as the small bits of grass and dirt fall back to the ground. Dust to dust. I carefully and precisely fold the small handkerchief, returning it to my purse. It is only now, as I stop talking, that I begin to listen. The whisper of wind in the leaves, the call of a distant bird, the whir of a lawn mower. I take comfort in these simple, mundane sounds, as the thought of my child lying here in empty silence breaks my heart. Closing my eyes, I lean my head back and take a deep, slow breath, the sun warming my face. A tenuous calm slowly returns to my mind and body with each breath. Opening my eyes, I smile down at where Maddy lies.

"I hope today you can find some peace. That all of us might find a little peace. I know that nothing will ever truly be enough, but perhaps after it is done we will move a step closer to justice. I hope that brings you some comfort... Do you even need comfort? Or are you protected from all of this, at peace no matter what happens today? For your sake, I hope so. Then, perhaps at least I can find some of that peace, resting in the knowledge that your killer is forever gone from this world, facing a judgment God alone can exact. Perhaps..."

Chapter 3

The reality of what is about to happen begins to sink in as I climb into a large van with the "Sheriff's Department" emblazoned on the side. After waiting for so many years, with delay after painful delay, it is suddenly upon me in a dizzying blur and I'm not sure I am ready for it. I can barely function; my nerves are so raw as Adam guides me into the vehicle with his firm arms around my shoulder, reaching across to buckle me in. I know that we just received instructions about what will happen in the coming few hours, but it is all suddenly gone. Again, Adam's presence is a comfort and I lean into him as the doors close and we pull out of the lot and onto the road. Within minutes, we are out of town and into the countryside, where I mutely watch the fields and trees fly by. Their gentle beauty stands in such stark contrast to what lies ahead that I shiver involuntarily. Someone behind us, a guard from the prison hands Adam a folded blanket, which he carefully wraps around my shoulders. I take his hand and squeeze it.

Avoiding the main gate, where media and protesters

have already begun to gather, we are rushed into the building and through security. I jump as the first set of barred doors slams shut behind us.

"Where's my purse?" I swing frantically around as I realize I am no longer carrying it.

"It's ok, Mom. We left it at security, remember? You won't need it." Nodding slowly, I vaguely remember the metal detectors and the guards who, despite knowing why I was there and doing their best to show compassionate respect, had still filled me with a sense of foreboding. I pat my side pocket, feeling the slight rise where I had put my folded handkerchief. Having taken it out of my purse, I kept it close to me, just in case—though the thought of shedding a single tear in front of the prisoner stiffens my resolve. We move slowly down a sterile hallway, turning a corner where the hall ends abruptly, with two doors, about ten feet apart, standing on the right-hand side. A guard opens the door for us, nervously gesturing for us to enter the room. I attempt to smile a thanks to him as we walk by, but look away when he smiles back, his eyes filled with a compassion I was not expecting. My throat constricts with emotion at this simple kindness. *Hold it together!* My knuckles whiten as my fists clench with determination.

After the intense brightness from the overhead fluorescent lighting in the halls, the subdued dimness of the room makes it feel like we are stepping into a small theatre. Two rows of upholstered chairs, the fabric pilled and frayed from time and use, face a large glass window on the wall opposite the door. Heavy curtains on the far side of the glass are pulled shut, blocking our view of the room beyond. The Death Room. During the briefing prior to arriving at the prison, the guard had used the name with such a casual familiarity that he might as well have been talking about the family living room. I cannot imagine what it would take for a person to get to a place where they can talk about that room in such an offhand way. It seems somehow... offensive, yet pitiable. All I know is that this room needs to be some kind of an end for me, a place of closure. I suppose we will soon find out.

"Mom," Adam whispers, gently directing me toward the front row. I must have been standing there for some time, as everyone is looking at me with that now-familiar expression of concern and pity. Again, I attempt a reassuring smile, patting his hand as it rests on my shoulder. We slowly move to the front row, taking our seats while a few others file in behind us. Adam and I are the only two in the front row, the empty chairs a reminder of those not present—Michael and Trevor. And Byron. Their absence weighs on me heavily, a confusing and overwhelming burden of anger, grief and longing. I had given the boys the freedom to decide whether or not to be here, but I want them here now. I cannot help but wonder: given the choice, would Byron be sitting here with me today? Or would he too have made me face this alone? It is only now that I realize how deeply I have resented my husband for leaving me alone to carry all of this for so long.

Fighting back the emotion, I drive these thoughts from my mind. I am not here for the boys or for Byron. I am not even here for myself. It isn't about us. This is about Maddy. Today I will bear witness on her behalf, stand in her place as the consequences of Mark's horrific choices are measured out upon him. He would finally face us one last time, no longer able to hide behind legal tactics and political maneuvering. He would face us as he is, a man convicted of the brutal murder of my child, and he would pay the final price for his crime. And then it would be finished.

A small movement at the edge of the window catches my eye. Slowly, the curtains are pulled back, one side at a time. The sudden brightness from the lights beyond makes us squint as our eyes adjust. And then the Death Room comes into focus. I am instantly struck by how small it is. Somehow I had expected something more, as though a room where such an important act of justice is meted out needs to be grand in scale and style. Instead, the small room reflects an institutional nakedness, a cold practicality, a clinical and sterile efficiency. And yet it is that very stark smallness that brings the gurney into such abrupt focus.

Situated in the center of the room, it is positioned at an angle, with the foot of the gurney pointing toward the right side of our viewing window. It is identical to what you would find in any hospital, with a few notable differences. The length of the gurney is fitted with half a dozen black restraints, resembling seat belts, to secure the prisoner from chest to feet. The most noteworthy exception, however, is the padded arm supports on each side, positioned at a slight angle from the length of the gurney. Each of these extensions is equipped with reinforced leather cuffs. Slightly nervous at the sight of so many restraints, I worry why they are necessary, but I am most uncomfortable with the almost cruciform shape the gurney presents. Refusing to be distracted by such thoughts, I continue to take in the scene before me.

The single guard in the room finishes the task of tying back the curtains he has just opened. Turning to the door near the head of the gurney, he quickly leaves the room, clearly self-conscious about his sudden audience. It is the only door in or out of the Death Room, the clock mounted above it ticking down the seconds. To the left of the door on the wall, an old rotary-style phone is affixed; its red plastic casing is muted with age, but still oddly vibrant in this sterile setting. We had a phone very much like this when Byron and I were first married, the kind with a metal bell inside that would ring tinnily whenever a call came in. That is a sound we do not want to hear today, not from that hated red phone, with the traitorous hope it offers a man who deserves none. My only comfort in seeing it is in knowing that our governor has never once commuted the sentence of a death row inmate—a fact he reiterated personally to me on the phone two days earlier. The red phone will not ring today. Still, I resent its presence in the room and look quickly away.

On the wall directly across from where we are seated is a mirror. Rather than being mounted on the wall, it is set into it like a window, which we know, in fact, that it is. It is from behind this two-way mirror that the executioner will administer the deadly mix of drugs to the prisoner. At the lower right corner of the mirror is a small square opening in the wall, through which two clear tubes have been passed, the ends of which are resting on a small tray covered in sterile fabric. Next to this is a monitor with sensors attached, ready to be applied. It is with this simple setup that Mark Williams will lose the life he forfeited his right to have for taking the life of my daughter, my Maddy. I've heard many people life say they wished they could push the plunger that would end Mark's life. Others have even suggested that it should be my right to do so. While I appreciate their somewhat over-zealous support, I am grateful that someone else is there to finish what has too long been left unfinished. I say a silent prayer of thanks for those men who are willing to serve justice in this way.

My heart jumps slightly in nervous anticipation as the door into the Death Room abruptly opens. I realize that in a matter of minutes, I will be facing the man who took my daughter and destroyed my family. What will he do when he sees us? Will he even look at me? Will he lash out in anger? Will I lash out at him? Adam tenses beside me, the hand on my arm tightening slightly. As I place my hand over his comfortingly, he relaxes, but only slightly. We watch as the warden enters the room shutting the heavy iron door behind him. Walking around the room, he inspects every detail, ensuring that everything is prepared and in order. He glances up at the clock above the door, then pulling back his sleeve, at the watch on his wrist. Again, to the clock, then he nods with grim satisfaction and turns to face us.

"Folks, I appreciate your patience. It will only be a minute or so before we begin." His voice comes through clearly into the room through a set of small speakers that I had not noticed before near the ceiling on either side of the large window, picked up by some unseen microphone in the Death Room. Stepping back, he bows his head as he waits with the rest of us. The seconds tick by, seeming to stretch on and on into a torturous eternity, when the door suddenly opens again. Two large guards enter first, one after the other, moving to either side of the door. That is when I see him.

Mark Allen Williams, wearing a faded prison jumpsuit, shuffles into the room, his hands and feet shackled. I feel as though the wind has been knocked out of me. His head is down, exposing the streaks of grey running through his dark hair. While I have seen him in court many times over the years, it has been some time since I have truly looked at him. I am almost startled by the contrast between the man standing before me and the idea of the killer I held in my head. So often my imagination had brought me back to that terrible night that I somehow still pictured Mark as the young man he was so many years ago. Instead, before me stands a middle-aged man whose features barely hint at the youth he once was. Raising his head, his pale skin and sunken cheeks betray the obvious anxiety and exhaustion of a man facing a premature death. And it is in this moment that I know justice has already started to be done. Watching him intently, my spine stiffens with resolve, sitting up straighter, refusing to be diminished in his presence, daring him to look back at me. And when he does look in my direction, our eyes lock.

What is that look on his face? He looks conflicted, as though he is being torn between shame and malice at seeing my face. Then, the hardness in his eyes softens. In defeat? Resignation? Or is that sadness? Uncomfortable now, I refuse to look away, trying impossibly to communicate in that brief glance a lifetime of grief and anger. And then, after that brief moment, he turns away and our eyes never meet again.

Turning away to the left, his face suddenly shows recognition and it collapses in grief. A painful sob bursts from his throat as he attempts to move in that direction, yet stops himself, looking quickly at the warden, who nods to the guards to let him step closer.

"It's ok, Mama," he manages to say, forcing a smile, "it's ok. Don't cry." It is only then that I realize there is another room next to ours, another window looking into the Death Room. I had known this, of course, as we had been assured that we would not encounter the "prisoner's witnesses," but with everything going on, I had not considered it again. Turning, I stared at the blank wall to my left, suddenly aware of the people so close, yet unseen. I hear a muffled sob, more through the glass than through the concrete wall, and I look away: Mark's mother weeping for her child. I had seen Lori Williams many times before, across the aisle in court or talking to the press on the front steps of the courthouse, though we've never spoken. I could never trust myself to speak to her, my anger so intense. After all, our children are what we raise them to be, and she had raised a murderer who had stolen my child. There was a time I might have dismissed her grief with contempt. She'd had years with Mark— years Maddy would never have—but finally she would know what it was like to have a child ripped from her forever. Yet, in this moment, I cannot summon the strength to hate her. Her grief is too much like my own, but while I can choose to let go of the anger I hold toward her, I cannot afford compassion. Not now. Not yet.

Looking away, I notice that another person has entered the room. A middle-aged man wearing wire-framed glasses and a clerical collar—a Catholic priest, I presume—stands near the gurney, his hands folded in front of a small, black leather-bound Bible. While his eyes never leave Mark, his lips seem to move slowly, his body rocking ever so slightly forward and backward. *He's praying*, I think to myself. Again, I remember having been told that the prisoner would be allowed a spiritual advisor with him. One of the guards walks around the priest, closing the door behind him. Everyone is now present. It is time.

With a deference I had not expected, the two guards

gently guide Mark away from the window where his mother is watching and lead him to the gurney. He sits, pulling himself up as far as he can, then pivots, lifting his feet—again with the help of the guards—so that he is able to lie flat. As the guards guide his hands to the arm supports, carefully but firmly securing him in place with the restraints, I notice that his hands are shaking. With practiced precision, the guards now begin to fasten the remaining body restraints, starting at his feet and working their way up to his chest. Finished, they step back as the warden approaches, inspecting every restraint with a gentle tug. The cold efficiency of every step in the process is both reassuring and disconcerting.

Apparently satisfied, the warden nods to the guards, who step forward, flanking our window, and quickly draw the curtains closed once more. *What's going on?* I think in panic, *will we suddenly be denied the justice that we had waited decades to receive?* Sensing the tension in my body, Adam leans closer, squeezing my shoulders.

"It's alright, Mom. We knew this was going to happen. They are just hooking him up to the monitor and attaching the IV to his arm. We don't get to see that part, but they'll open the curtain the moment they're done." He's right, of course, and I let the tension drain from my rigid body—some of it, anyway. Settling back into my seat, I try to imagine what is happening on the other side of the curtain, try to picture the process required to prepare a man to die. We don't wait long; the curtains are drawn back open again in a matter of minutes. Having secured the curtains on each side, the two guards turn and leave the room. Mark jumps at the sound of the heavy door shutting behind them, the heart monitor silently registering the jump in his heart rate through sensors taped to his chest. The IV lines that run through the small square hole in the far wall are now taped cleanly in place to his arm, as though he is here simply to donate blood.

Leaning down, the priest whispers something into Mark's ear, who nods slowly as he closes his eyes, tears running down his stubbled cheek. Stepping back to make room for the warden to take his place, the priest places a comforting hand on Mark's bound lower leg, where it will stay for the remainder of his time in the Death Room.

"Do you have any final words, Mark?" asks the warden. Another surge of dread courses through me, my body tensing. This time, there is no comforting reassurance from Adam, whose own body is equally coiled with the same tension.

"I want to say to my family, to my mama—Mama? I love you so much." Mark's voice wavers as he speaks, turning his head toward the unseen room to our left. "Don't let this beat you, ok? Remember what I told you before—don't let hate into your heart. You gotta forgive them, Mom. Not just for their sake, but for yours. I love you!" He turns now to face the invisible men behind the two-way mirror who will end his life. "I want to say that I forgive you for what you have to do to me today. I forgive you too, warden. I know you're just doing your job.

"I want to say that I am innocent." He doesn't look our way, but I know he is addressing us. "I didn't do the awful thing you think I did. I loved Maddy and I could never have hurt her. This is wrong, but I hope you can find some peace after today." Hearing her name on his lips is a bitter slap to the face.

"Just do it, already!" Adam hisses through clenched teeth. No one can hear him except for me. My heart breaks at what this is costing my son. *Yes, let this be over, please.*

After a moment of silence, Mark takes a deep breath, then turns to the warden and nods: "That's all, sir. Thank you, warden." Taking a deep breath, he turns his face toward the ceiling. With that, the warden looks into the two-way mirror and nods, his face emotionless and stern. Again, a sense of panic rushes through my entire body as I watch the IV lines shift slightly. Will I be able to see the liquid as it runs through the line into Mark's body? Has it already started? It is as though time is slowing, stopping, yet the steady rise and fall of Mark's chest rhythmically marks the passage of every second. And then, that too begins to slow. His eyes droop, then close entirely, as though he is simply drifting off into a gentle sleep. The silence screams in my ears as I watch every movement in his bound body, not willing even to look at the heart monitor. However, such a look is unnecessary, as he becomes absolutely still.

It is finished.

He is gone. Mark Williams is dead. The man who stole our daughter from us and plunged our lives into a living hell no longer draws breath on this earth. At this realization, all the tension drains from my body without warning and I feel as though I am going to slide from my chair and collapse onto the floor. Yet, I remain where I am, my eyes fixed on his body, as the guards redundantly check for a pulse despite the flatline displayed on the heart monitor.

What is it that I am feeling? Is it relief? Perhaps closure? No, nothing so final, nothing so black and white. Instead, there is an emptiness in my heart where an abiding anger had so long been rooted, but now is gone, leaving only traces of itself behind, like echoes. The emptiness aches, but it also carries with it the promise or at least the possibility of being filled with something else. With something better than what has been there for so long.

"Time of death is 6:17pm."

PART II
LORI

Chapter 1

I f there's a way to be prepared to be called the "Monster's Mother", no one told me.

Of course, no one has ever said it to my face—only the faceless shout from the crowd outside the courthouse—but it was there, the unspoken accusation in the eyes of so many people. While it would start to die down as time passed, with every new hearing, news report or attempt at appeal—every time I stepped into the spotlight in order to save my son's life—it would spark back to life. Will today finally be an end to it, once and for all? Perhaps, but it doesn't really matter much in the end. People can call me whatever they want; they can insinuate the worst things about my character, my capacity as a parent, but it won't change a thing. I will never be ashamed to be his mother.

Sitting on the edge of the bed, I draw in a long breath and release it slowly in an exhausted sigh. I don't regret a single moment spent in fighting for my son's life—what mother would?—but it is just that it has been so very hard for so very long. Would anyone blame me for stopping now? Surely every bit of hope has proven itself false, so why demand more of myself than the broken scales of justice have ever offered? I've made it this far, to *this* day, yet sitting here now I am not sure if I have any more to give. I am not sure I even have the strength to get up off this bed. And then I do, leaning forward, pushing myself to my feet. How many times have I been here before, with nothing more to give, yet getting up nonetheless? What other choice do I have? Today is no different than any of the others, but perhaps tomorrow will be.

All along the narrow hallway of the apartment, rows of school photos line the wall, from the enthusiasm of Mark's kindergarten picture through the awkward "smile-but-be-cool" high school smirks. He used to refer to it as the wall of shame, especially when we had guests over. I laugh to myself at the thought, smiling back at each of Mark's happy faces, every one smiling back at me. I am tempted to stay here among these moments of joy, preserved forever, but again, I will myself forward into what the day holds.

In truth, those pictures don't tell the true story, but like for most people, they represent the pretense of a happiness not always as real as we hope for. His last few years of high school were especially difficult for Mark—and for me. His grades began to drop, he started hanging out with the boys I'd have preferred him to avoid, and he would stay out until all hours of the night, getting up to God knows what. We'd always been close but without warning he became distant, sullen and angry. I tried everything I thought might help to coax him back to himself, but all I ended up doing was nagging him to get his act together. I hoped it was nothing more than typical teenage rebellion, but the first time the police brought him home, I knew things were more serious than I had been willing to admit. Drunk, Mark and some friends had been picked up for disturbing the peace. He would have been let off with a warning, but apparently he had taken a swing at one of the officers. Thankfully he was too drunk to actually connect with his target, a young officer whose mother attended our church, so he was spared formal charges. The officer nodded politely to my thanks but warned me that Mark would not likely be this lucky a second time. He was right, of course, and I found myself at the police station a half-dozen times over the next six months.

Refusing to let my son throw his life away, I confronted him, levelling an ultimatum: shape up or get out. Of course, he would likely have opted for the second option had his uncles not been there to keep him from running off. In the end, however, he was willing to try. First things first: I needed to keep him in school so that he could graduate, which meant I would need to hire a tutor to get him back on track. When the school recommended several programs which I couldn't afford, one of his teachers recommended a student tutor. That's how I met Madeline. She was the sweetest thing—polite, confident and sharp as a tack! Having tutored several other students in grades below her, she was unsure if Mark would accept a peer in the same grade as his tutor. However, she was willing to try and I assured her that I would *make* him accept this.

To my pleasant surprise, Mark didn't take any convincing at all. In truth, I'm not sure he needed a tutor at all—he was a smart kid, always had been. Yet, having someone to keep him accountable, to make up ground he'd lost over the year, and to encourage him seemed to be what he needed most. It was as though I was finally getting my son back. Slowly, Mark became himself again:

his grades improving, his playful attitude reemerging and spending less time with those so-called *friends* of his. In fact, he was spending most of his free time with Madeline. I didn't doubt that it was more than her skills as a tutor that kept my boy interested- she was a beautiful girl, after all—but it soon became clear that the interest was mutual. Nervous at first, I cautioned him to be careful, to focus on his studies, but I soon began to relax. Maddy was a good girl who was helping my son become a better man. When they came into the apartment one afternoon holding hands, I couldn't have been happier.

I flick the button on the electric kettle as I walk into the kitchen, grabbing a mug and tea bag while it begins to click and hiss to life. I'd given up coffee years ago, finding it hard enough to sleep after all that had happened. While I'd never considered myself a tea person, Maddy had started me drinking it when she would hang around our place. Leaning against the counter now, I try to picture the three of us here in the kitchen, Maddy and I sipping our tea, Mark chugging a cola while teasing us for drinking that "muddy water". It's hard to imagine those happier days now, lost in so many years, so much pain and grief poisoning my memories. Yet, the image remains, the sound of our laughter a fading echo that lingers in this too-empty kitchen even now, twenty years later.

They had started to hang out at our apartment more and more often, with Maddy becoming a familiar guest at our small dinner table. When I asked about her family, it was clear that she loved her parents and brothers a lot. Then I asked what her folks thought about her and Mark dating. The two of them exchanged a nervous look before answering.

"Oh, my little brother is going through a tough time

right now, so they have too much on their hands. When things settle down, I'm sure they'll love Mark as much as I do." Love! I was as surprised by how easily she said it as I was by how *unsurprised* Mark was to hear it. This relationship was clearly more serious than I had thought. I was so pleased that my son had found himself such a wonderful, responsible young woman that I completely forgot their evasiveness about her parents. I was sure I would meet them eventually.

The first time I spoke to Maddy's parents was early on the day after she hadn't returned home. They were calling everyone they knew in search of their missing girl. One of Madeline's friends, who knew she and Mark were dating, had given them our phone number. I could hear the panic in Alice Goodman's voice as she asked if we had seen their daughter. I assured her that I hadn't, but that I would ask Mark if he knew where she was. Putting down the phone, I hurried down the hall to his room. Would he be in his room at all? Was he somewhere with her? I began to worry as I knocked on his door, trying the handle only to find it locked. Then it struck me: she was probably in there with him. Dammit, if that boy got her pregnant... A moment later, Mark opened the door, rubbing at his eyes, clearly having just been asleep.

"What the hell, Ma?" he moaned, annoyed at having been woken up so early.

"Mark, do you know where Maddy is?" I asked, glancing over his shoulder to his empty bed. He stared at me blankly as I asked the question. "Her mother is on the phone. She didn't come home last night. Do you know where she is?"

"What?" He was now fully alert. "I just saw her last

night. We hung out until, like, two in the morning. I know, I know, I was out past curfew, but—"

"Don't worry about that right now. Come talk to Mrs. Goodman. She's on the phone." We made our way back to the living room, where Mark picked up the phone.

"Hello? Yes, ma'am, this is Mark... No, ma'am, I've not seen her since last—" He stopped, interrupted by Maddy's mother. "Yes, we were together last night... I walked her most of the way home... Well, it was late... Close to two in the morning. She was fine when—" I could hear Alice Goodman's raised voice through the phone, even from a few feet away. "Yes, ma'am. Can you let me know if you—" He pulled the receiver from his ear and stared at it. Turning to me he said, "She hung up."

The rest of the day was a slow torture for both of us as we waited for any news. Mark was beside himself with worry, and while I assured him she was probably fine, that it would all be cleared up soon enough, I began to doubt my own words. The worst was not knowing. Mark wanted to go look for her, but I convinced him to stay, telling him that if Maddy was OK, she would call or come here to the apartment sooner or later. Grudgingly he agreed, spending the rest of the day pacing like a caged animal. When the police arrived later that afternoon to get a statement from Mark, he was desperate to help in any way possible. Agreeing to come down to the station, he began to leave with the officers. I insisted on driving him myself, but Mark begged me to stay home in case Maddy showed up or called. To this day, I regret letting my son leave without me.

As I stand here, rehearsing the memories again for the thousandth time, a weight settles on my shoulders. After not hearing from Mark in hours, I rushed down to the station where I was made to wait. As his mother, I wanted to be there to support Mark as he gave his statement. However, I soon learned that Mark was not actually giving a statement at all, but was being questioned. Having recently turned eighteen, I was informed that I had no parental rights to be present during Mark's interrogation. *Interrogation*. When the clerk at the counter used that word, I knew that everything had changed.

The next day, Mark was charged with Maddy's murder. *My son was accused of killing his girlfriend, the woman he loved so deeply*. Without warning, we were swept away into a chaos of accusations, tests, appeals and threats. We later learned that the success of defending against a murder charge like this is often measured on how you respond in those critical first few hours. Yet, it seems that every attempt I had made to protect my son's interests were met with a systematic effort to thwart our success. So sure were the authorities of my son's guilt that his supposed "presumption of innocence" seemed to be dismissed as irrelevant or even offensive in the face of Maddy's death. *Maddy was dead*. No matter how hard I fought to protect Mark from an increasingly inevitable and devastating outcome, he could not fight for himself. Completely lost in grief and shock, he began to shut down. Yet even this was taken as evidence of his guilt.

I have never admitted this out loud to anyone, but in those darkest moments, I began to have doubts. *What if...?* The sickening fear began to whisper uncertainties to me. *What if Mark* did *kill Madeline? What if I am blinded to the truth by my love for my son? By an unwillingness to face the truth?* I asked Mark once—and only once—if he had done it. The disbelieving despair that came over his face at my question made me regret this traitorous betrayal. Doubts be damned! My son was not a killer. How could I even consider such a thing?

Yet, how could I not at least ask the question? After all, what parent wants to believe that their child is capable of murder? I knew that Mark was not perfect, that he'd made his fair share of mistakes, perhaps even worse than most. His police record certainly didn't paint a good picture, but weighed against his whole life, against the last few months, surely people could see that he was far more than the caricature being drawn by the investigators, the prosecution, and the media. I tried my best to be the parent he needed, but I know that I wasn't able to do everything. Being the single mother of a teenaged boy wasn't easy. Not that I am making excuses. I accept my share of the blame and responsibility for Mark's mistakes. Yet there is a huge difference between being a troubled kid in a single-parent family and being a cold-blooded killer.

Sadly, such a distinction was dismantled systematically for the jury. Those not convinced by his "questionable character" had decided that, since Mark was the last person to admit seeing Maddy alive, and since his DNA was discovered on her body (easily explained by their romantic relationship), he was *guilty beyond a reasonable doubt*. And the press ate up the manufactured details, spinning a chilling tale of an innocent honour-role student taken advantage of and ultimately murdered by a violent thug with a history of crime. And so Mark was sentenced to death by lethal injection, with a cold and clinical efficiency.

Glancing at the clock, I realize that I am going to be late if I don't leave now. My brothers offered to drive me, but I wanted to be alone, so I told them that I would meet them there. However, left to my own devices, I had lost track of time. I don't even have enough time to finish my tea. *Time.* After the finality of Mark's sentence, it seemed that time was all we had. Grateful for every moment he remained alive, it was also a kind of cruel torture as, year after year, we waited with dread for the day they would kill my son. While no one suffered as much as Mark, who had begun to retreat into himself again, no one in our life was untouched by this agony. Family and friends, people in our church, and those who had become involved in the campaign to save him—everyone showed the signs of stress and trauma from the delay. *Cruel and unusual.* These words are so obviously true in cases like this that it baffles me to this day how people can deny that they describe the true nature of the death penalty.

I hope that today, somehow, people will begin to see this truth. I know that if it is going to happen, I will have a part to play. *Dear Jesus, give me the strength and wisdom.* Grabbing my keys, I head out the door, terrified but determined to face what lies ahead.

Chapter 2

After so many years of visiting my son in prison —passing through endless security checkpoints, locked behind sliding doors of heavy iron bars, and having hushed conversations through phones with safety glass between us—I have still not gotten used to how quickly and easily I can visit him now. After all, there are no guards at the cemetery. I can visit Mark whenever I want, only now there is no phone receiver where I can hear his voice, no glass through which I can see his face. It is bitter-sweet to stand here now, grateful that my boy is no longer wasting away in that awful prison, yet crushed by the price that such a freedom exacted on him, on all of us. The polished granite of his gravestone seems entirely untouched, despite having been here for a full cycle of the seasons already, his name etched with precision.

Mark Allen Williams

Beloved Son, Free At Last

I take comfort in the enduring and intact nature of the stone, preferring to look at it than to consider what remains of my son only a few feet beneath where I am standing now. I shiver involuntarily at the thought. No, that is not my son, not really. I know that he is in a better place. At first, when such sentiments were shared at his funeral, I was too angry to hear them, dismissing them bitterly as empty words meant to distract me from the painful injustice irrevocably done to Mark. Yet, at the funeral, I had been moved by the words of Father Jim, the priest who served as Mark's spiritual advisor and who stood with him at the execution. With a practiced remembrance, he recited the Scripture without needing to open his small Bible:

"We do not live to ourselves, and we do not die to ourselves. If we live, we live to the Lord, and if we die, we die to the Lord; so then, whether we live or whether we die, we are the Lord's. For to this end Christ died and lived again, so that he might be Lord of both the dead and the living."

In that moment, when those words broke through my anger, I finally began to grieve for the son lost to me—no, taken from me. And I wept. When the interment was over and everyone had left me for a few last minutes alone at the grave, Father Jim laid a gentle hand of comfort on my shoulder and turned to leave. I quickly took his hand, wordlessly asking him to remain with me. And so we stood there together in silence, looking down on the man who had meant so much to both of us.

A Baptist my entire life, I had been somewhat taken aback when Mark became Catholic in prison. When he introduced me to Father James Hamilton, SJ—who insisted we call him Father Jim—I had initially been suspicious, wondering if he had taken advantage of my son's vulnerability in order to convert him. However, it soon became clear that Mark had found something he needed in his newfound faith, some peace through his friendship with this balding Jesuit with the easy smile. Assuring me that we were "still part of the same team", Mark explained to me that Father Jim had helped him learn how to trust God, even on death row. When he began to emerge from his dark depression and begin to find joy in life—even if only a little—my suspicion turned to gratitude. When we came to making funeral arrangements for Mark, a task no parent should ever have to do for their child, our family church was very understanding that he wanted a Catholic service. To his credit, Father Jim found ways to integrate my pastor and our church into the service. He continues to be an important friend and spiritual support to me.

In fact, it was Father Jim who had encouraged me to visit Mark's grave as often as I needed to, encouraging me to talk to him, to say anything I felt I necessary. While I had so much to say to Mark, I could not bring myself to do it, not here. I wanted to remember my son in places where he truly lived—in our home, in his old bedroom or in the kitchen where we'd have so many chats over the years— but not in this place. To do so reminded me too vividly of all the bad that had happened, the dark end to Mark's precious life. Frustrated, I explained to Father Jim that, despite needing to visit that spot, I could not talk to Mark. Smiling patiently, the priest made another suggestion.

"That's perfectly understandable, Lori. Maybe you can talk to God instead. Talk to him about Mark, about anything. There aren't any rules here, you know." While it had been strange at first, it soon became an important part of my week, a time of peaceful prayer that brought hope and meaning into this place of mourning, yet still left room for the grief I would always carry in my heart.

Here now, I need that peace more than ever. Today I need to pour out to God all the raw, uncensored feelings in my heart, especially with what I will be facing later today.

"Oh, Jesus," I say, my words burdened by the sweet and unrelenting obligation of motherhood, "I need your strength for today, for what I am about to face. I thought that knowing this day was coming would help me be prepared for what is expected of me, but now, with the time at hand, I don't know what I will do—what I *should* do. Haven't I done enough? What possible good can come from any of this anyway? Mark is gone! It can't be *undone*. Forgiveness or retribution—can either bring back the child so horrifically stolen from me? Why should I pay the price, yet again? I know that it is not just about me—trust me, I've known that it hasn't been about me for a long time now- but maybe it's my turn? Can it be about me, just for today?" My body is shaking, my fists clenched at my sides as I look up into the sky, into the invisible face of God. But he is silent, the cloud impassively drifting across the distant blue. Taking a deep breath, I try to calm myself.

"Do you know that people have actually been coming up to me and congratulating me. *Congratulating!* Can you imagine? 'Your boy will finally get justice,' they say. 'Too little, too late,' I want to reply, but of course I don't. People say the stupidest things sometimes, but I can't judge them. I'd probably say the same things if I were in their place, at least before all of this happened to us. The comment that makes me the most angry is when people say, 'God is making all things right now, Lori.' It makes me want to scream at them, 'If God is able to make things right, why did he wait until now?'

"It's a fair question, isn't it? Why *didn't* you do something sooner? It's bad enough that we can't trust our so-called justice system, at the very least we should be able to rely on you, the all-powerful and loving God, right? You know that Mark was falsely accused, railroaded in the investigation, robbed of a fair trial, and suffering for years on death row awaiting a sentence of death for a murder he did not—could not!—have committed. At any point in that process, couldn't you have intervened? Uncovered evidence or persuaded the jury? Anything! Yet, you did nothing. Nothing! Only then, after it is too late to save Mark from any of this, the real killer comes forward, confessing of his own free will. Suddenly, everyone who so quickly condemned my son is scrambling to 'make things right'. Is *this* your justice? Well, *dear Lord*," I say venomously, "you can take your justice and choke on it!"

My heart is racing, anger pumping through my veins with an intensity I have not felt in a long time. Again, I force myself to breathe, to take control of the emotions that wash over me like a tsunami. Talking to God in this way would have been enough to get me the strap as a child. You did not yell at God. You did not blame him. He is right and we are wrong. *Period.* Yet, Father Jim has helped me learn to accept these outbursts. We can't always pray like that, he told me, but sometimes those are the most honest and authentic prayers we can offer to God. If he's right, I'm being more *authentic* than ever. This thought makes me chuckle at myself, breaking the tension in my body, my shoulders loosening, my fists opening. Now it is time to listen, to give God his turn, letting him speak into the silence.

And it is in that silence that I remember one of the last things Mark ever said to me. On the day of his execution, we were able to visit him one last time. Unlike previous visits, this one was in a small room where we were allowed to embrace, something I had not done to my son in many years. I was grateful for this small mercy on that day we were to say goodbye. Before I knew it, our time was over and I was filled with dread and anger. With a sob, I said to Mark that I hated what was being done to him, that I hated the *people* responsible for it. With a compassion and gentleness that I could not fathom, my son took my hand and shook his head. He looked me in the eyes and said something I will never forget.

"Ma, I need you to make me a promise, OK? I need you to promise me that you won't hate. No, listen to me. If anyone has the right to hate the people responsible for all of this, it's me—and God knows I've wanted to! But I don't, Mom. I don't hate them and neither should you. Don't blame the Goodman's for this. They only did what they thought was right, what they believed they had to do for Maddy. Think about what they lost. You can understand that, right? What *wouldn't* you have done for me if you were in that position? Don't give me that look, Ma. You know exactly what I mean. Be angry! Fight this fucked up system to your dying breath; if not for me then for all the other guys here on the row. Be angry, fight, but please, *please* don't hate. It'll kill you, Ma. Promise me, ok?"

And I had promised him—how could I refuse him anything in that moment?—yet I had no idea what such a promise would cost me in the end. In the midst of my anger in this moment, Mark's words and the promise that I made him come into my mind. Impossibly, Mark had made peace with what had happened to him. He had no more insight into why God had not intervened, why such injustice was allowed to happen in the world, yet he was able to face that injustice with a grace I could not begin to imagine. He had chosen forgiveness. I am still not sure I can make that choice or even if I understand what it means to do so.

"OK, God, I need your help. I made a promise to my son and I need you to help me keep that promise. I will not let my memories of Mark be corrupted by hatred, but I will need you to give me whatever it was that you gave him. Father Jim calls you the 'God of the impossible.' Well, now is your chance to prove it, especially today. I need that grace. I need wisdom. I need your words because my own are poisoned with unforgiving anger. Your will, not mine, be done."

Opening my eyes slowly, I blink against the sudden brightness of the sun as it emerges from behind a cloud, its rays warming my face. Did it work? Am I somehow different? My boiling anger has cooled to a simmer, but I know how quickly that can change. I guess I will have to wait and see what happens when I arrive at the court-house. Turning, I begin to walk back to where I had parked my car. It is finally time.

"Amen."

Chapter 3

The judge's face furrows as he gathers various papers on the bench in front of him, tapping them firmly on the desk to force them into some semblance of order. I'm late, slipping into the back of the courtroom and settling into the seat Father Jim has saved for me. I smile and take his hand, grateful for his support. I spot my brothers, three rows ahead, sitting with their wives. All four turn, and seeing me, offer apologetic looks for the lack of seating. My oldest brother, Phil, points at his watch to remind me that I should have been here earlier. I nod to them that I understand, and they turn back to face the front. I take a deep breath. I'm here, and it's time.

The judge scans the room, as though looking for something particular. Or *someone*, it would seem. His narrowed, searching eyes eventually find me, open with recognition, and linger there for just a moment. While the expression on his face does not change in the slightest, his eyes seem to soften as they meet my own. With a quick nod, as though he has just settled something he had not been sure of, he looks away. Clearing his throat, he addresses the court:

"There is a certain responsibility that judges bear when dealing with cases in which the victims have suffered in particularly troubling ways, especially victims of violent crimes. This is most notably true in capital cases, where the sentence of death by execution is a possible outcome—a sentence, I must admit, that I am prone to enforce in this case, given the uniquely egregious nature of the crime and all that has happened since. I believe the victims deserve the most unequivocal justice we can provide. This is true of those who are the direct victim of these crimes, but it is also true of all those who have been negatively impacted by the crimes, especially friends and loved ones. They are victims too, and while the law is perhaps inadequate in addressing their suffering, we must make every effort to see that they receive justice as well. This case, however, has exposed to me the often uncomfortable truth that the family and friends of the offender can also become victims of these crimes. They, too, deserve to receive justice, no matter how complex and difficult it is to do so.

"This is why I believe in the importance of victim impact statements in this process. These statements are essential, not only in order to allow the victims the right to have their stories heard and made part of the official record, but because I am able to take such statements into consideration prior to deciding on a sentence. Understand, there is no legal obligation for me to change my decisions based upon these statements, but I believe that I am bound by a moral obligation to consider them, to integrate them into my final judgment. To that end, I urge everyone who decides to give such a statement here today to take this privilege seriously.

"I admit that this case—the murder of Madeline Goodman—has me deeply troubled, for many reasons. Not the least of which is the fact that a court in this state has already tried one man for that crime, finding him guilty and rendering upon his body the harshest penalty our system can offer: death. Even as we sit here, the state is investigating what went wrong—and, well, something clearly *did* go wrong because Mark Williams died for a crime we now know he did not commit. While it is not my role here today to comment on those events, I want to make it part of the record that I condemn that travesty of justice, and I hope that anyone complicit in that debacle will face judgment themselves.

"Without question, the defendant's confession allows us to correct something of the injustices perpetuated thus far, taking us that much closer to the justice young Madeline deserves. Yet, because it comes too late, it bears the culpability of another life irretrievably lost. I cannot and will not praise this willing confession that came after two decades of cowardly silence. Neither am I inclined toward any degree of leniency in my sentencing. And so, it is only in the statements we will hear today that any hope of mercy lies.

"Mark Williams is not legally acknowledged as a victim here today, yet he is, without question, a victim whose death is no less final and devastating than Madeline Goodman's. Therefore, I have decided that, under these unique circumstances, the family of Mark Williams will be allowed to make a victim impact statement here today." Again, the judge's eyes find me in at the back of the room. "Mrs. Williams, it is my understanding that you have agreed to make such a statement to the court today. Is that correct?"

"It is, your honor," I say, standing nervously, legs suddenly weak beneath me.

"Lori Williams is the mother of Mark Williams," the judge informs the room matter-of-factly. "Mrs. Williams, please feel free to use the microphone set up on the right side of the courtroom."

With a reassuring squeeze on the shoulder from Father Jim, I stand up. Every eye in the room follows me as I make my way to where the microphone is set up near the prosecution's desk. Those eyes that once watched me with condemnation and scorn now seem filled with curiosity and pity. Ignoring all but the supportive looks of my family and friends, I continue toward the front, where the microphone and a small wooden podium stand. I nervously rest my hands on the bare podium; I made no notes for today. At this very moment, I do not know what I am going to say.

Allowing me a sweeping view of the room, the microphone is situated on the right side of the space. I keep my eyes on the judge, knowing that a simple turn of my head will bring me into a direct line of sight with the defendant's table, where the person responsible for both Mark's and Maddy's deaths awaits judgment. I will face him—I know that I must—but not yet. I am not ready. And so I look to the judge, who nods for me to begin. Nodding back, I offer him a weak smile, his words having touched me deeply. I clear my throat and take a deep, steadying breath.

"It has only been one year since my son, Mark, was killed, put to death for a crime he did not commit. In truth, his life was taken from him more than twenty years ago. He was just at the beginning of his life, his future ahead of him as he was starting to become the man I knew he could be. And then he was locked away like an animal. In those first years in prison, he refused to give up hope, believing that truth and justice must win out in the end, that he would be freed. Even after he was sentenced to death, he refused to let go of the hope that it must have been a random chance, an unlucky fluke of an otherwise trustworthy system. Yet, when the weeks became months and the months became years, that hope was crushed out of him, out of us both. In its place cynicism and despair took root, and the boy that I loved withdrew into himself, becoming an empty shell of what he once was, a shadow of the promise of what he might have become. It has been one year since my boy was killed, but it was as though his soul had died long ago and his body was simply waiting to catch up.

"I watched helplessly as Mark slipped away. And while I can never compare my suffering with what he went through, my own soul began to fall apart, too. Mark was all that I had, my only child. He was my whole world, my life. To lose a child is any parent's worst fear, yet never in my darkest nightmares had I imagined a loss like this. When he was convicted of Maddy's murder, his whole life was erased. In it, his entire story was rewritten; he was branded a troubled youth with the cold heart of a killer. And I became the mother of a murderer, the mother of the monster, some suggesting that my own hands were stained with blood. I tried to ignore it, to live my life as best I could, supporting my son in the process, but it became impossible. The simple act of shopping for groceries required driving across town where I hoped I would not be recognized, confronted, and judged.

"Every spare moment of my life was consumed by trials, appeals, and endless paperwork, all while trying to make ends meet. I lost my job because I had taken too many days off, though I know they had been looking for an excuse to let me go since the case went public. If it were not for the help of my family and my church, I would have lost my apartment. And yet, through all of this, I needed to keep up the face of optimism and hope for Mark's sake. If he had known what I was suffering, it would have destroyed him, so I kept on smiling and promising hope. In time, things stabilized, but I will probably never recover all that I lost, a lifetime of hard work, careful planning and what little I'd saved to retire on.

"And then, at the end of it all, I watched my only child executed—no, *murdered*—before my very eyes!" I can feel my blood begin to surge again, as the anger I felt early starts to rise in me. I try to speak, but the words are choked with emotion and I am forced to stop, to look down, closing my eyes. *Breathe, Lori. Just breathe.* Slowly, some semblance of peace returns. "There is nothing that can prepare a mother to watch her child killed. It is the most inhuman form of torture ever imagined. No one- *no one!*- should ever be subjected to that kind of cruelty."

For the first time, I turn and face the defendant's table. Yet, it is not his face that I look for. I look past him, behind him in the gallery to where his family sits, their faces masks of utter brokenness and shock, a state that I am all too familiar with. I find the eyes of the woman who sat across the aisle from me in so many previous visits to this court, yet whose eyes I've looked into only one time before this day. On that day, her eyes had been filled with accusation and grief, a steely anger that seemed to dare me to speak to her. Yet today those eyes are filled with tears,

tears of desperation and shame. More than that, what I see now in the eyes of Alice Goodman is a desperate plea, a longing hope that I can extend to her what she once refused me.

When I consider the truth about what really happened that night, I want to deny her that small mercy. The news that Maddy's brother, Trevor, had come forward and confessed to the murder, had left me in shock. Mark's lawyer, who was herself in shock over this news, managed to find out more details and recounted for us what Trevor's confession had revealed.

The night that Maddy had gone missing, she had left Mark at two in the morning, heading home on a shortcut through the woods behind her parents home. I remember Mark saying that he had wanted to walk her home, but that she had insisted she was fine; it was only a ten-minute walk on a path she'd taken a thousand times before. It was in those woods that she came across Trevor with some other young guys. As his friends left, Madeline had confronted her brother, recognizing one of the others as a drug dealer. He was already high and they had begun to argue. At one point, Maddy had wrestled the drugs from Trevor's pocket, throwing them as far she could into the forest. In the heat of the moment, blinded by a drug-induced rage, he picked up a rock and struck his sister on the head, killing her. After groping in the dark until he had found the discarded drugs, he fled the scene, leaving her there to be found the next day.

As I imagine her lifeless body left there in the woods, my heart breaks for her all over again. I know that I am speaking here today as much for Maddy as I am for Mark.

"When I learned that Madeline's brother had confessed, I was gripped with an irrational hope that this news could somehow save my son, somehow undo what could never be undone. And when I realized that, if this uselessly late confession had come just a few weeks earlier, it would have saved Mark's life, was uselessly too late, all I wanted was for *that* man to die. Oh yes, all of my carefully argued convictions about why the death penalty needs to be abolished were gone. I simply did not care. Unlike Mark, this man had not only brutally murdered his own sister over a small bag of heroin, he had let my only child die for it. If you had asked me then what I would say to you today, it would be that this monster deserves to die and that I want to be there to watch it happen!"

For the first time, I look directly at Trevor, the man responsible for my son's death. His pale, emaciated face stares blankly at the table in front of him, seemingly oblivious to the words I have just spoken. The anger flares inside me again. *Does he even care? Does he even have a soul? What kind of monster can be so callous?*

Even as I think this, I remember that same look of empty resignation on Mark's face as he sat in that same chair so many years ago. And it was that same expression that others took as evidence of his cold, soulless nature, and thus, obvious guilt. A sob escapes my lips as compassion breaks into my chest without warning, compassion for this poor, broken man I thought I hated. The tears are now flowing down my cheeks as I turn back toward the judge.

"Trevor Goodman deserves to pay for his crimes, both for the death of his sister, Maddy, and the death of my son, Mark. Two lives have been needlessly lost and justice must be served. Yet, to sentence him to death would simply return evil for evil. It would be saying that what he was in that moment is all that ever will be, that he could never be anything more than a user and a killer." I shake my head sadly.

"To accept that would be a betrayal of the very people whose deaths we are seeking to find justice for. The year before Mark was arrested, his life was falling apart too—a fact the prosecution and the press did not hesitate to exploit. If something hadn't changed, he might very well have been in the same place Trevor was before long. Yet, in those short months when he and Maddy were together, something changed in him. Maddy loved Mark, and her unwavering belief that he was more than his worst mistakes was what convinced him to start making better choices. He began to see himself through her eyes, and she saw not what he had done nor how he might fail, but rather, she saw the possibilities of what he might achieve, what he might become. I believe she held this same hope for her brother too. And so, it would betray her to deny Trevor the opportunity she died trying to give him.

"Again, Trevor Goodman deserves to pay for his crimes. However, I have to believe that justice is not simply about getting what we deserve, but that *true justice* is to be found in the love that drove Maddy to help my son and to try and help her brother. I have to believe that it is *that* kind of justice that can reach into the brokenness that these crimes have inflicted on so many of us, regardless of which side of the courtroom we find ourselves on, and do its imperfect best to restore us all. Taking another life, creating yet more victims lost to this horrible crime—how will this do anything other than to leave us all that much more broken? It must end here.

"Trevor," My throat tightens as I address him directly for the first time, "There is no way I could ever make you understand the kind of pain and suffering you have caused me. I want nothing more than to see you feel something of that pain if only it would *make* you understand. My son wanted something different for me, and he wanted something different for you too. He didn't know that you were the one who had taken Maddy's life, but he had somehow found a way to forgive you. He made me promise to forgive you too, a promise I intend to keep, even if I cannot do that here and now. Perhaps I never will. Or perhaps, I will come to discover that mysterious grace my son had. It's going to take time, maybe even a lifetime. Perhaps for you too. In the end, I hope that we both find the peace we need."

Without another word, I turn from the podium and begin to walk back toward my seat. The court has fallen into complete silence. As I move toward the center aisle, I find that Alice Goodman has made her way there. She watches me nervously as I approach, and my own heart skips a beat as I pause in front of her. Tentatively, she reaches her trembling hand toward me, and all I can do is stare at it, the gulf between us suddenly vast. *I can't do this. It's too much! It's too soon! Hasn't this been enough?*

And then, I reach out and take her hand in mine, just for a moment. And that gulf between us closes—not completely, but enough. Perhaps in time...

THE END

BEYOND THE LAST VERDICT

Since 1976, there have been more than 1400 state sanctioned executions in the United States. That is three people a month for 40 years. And this says nothing of the countless other men and women who wait for their execution day, on average for 15 years after conviction, with some waiting years longer. While the number of people executed in the US each year is on the decline—from 295 in 1998 to 49 in 2015—there are still nearly 3000 people on death row.

And 2015 saw a new record in the American justice system, with nearly 150 people exonerated for wrongful convictions, with an average prison stay of 14 years. Consider that: the number of years wasted in prison from the lives of innocent people in 2015 alone is well over 2000 years. That is just one year and only those who were exonerated—and let's face it, if 150 were exonerated, we can be assured that there were many innocent people who were not.

It doesn't end there. According to the Equal Justice Initiative:

"A record 58 people were exonerated in homicide cases last year, including five people who had been sentenced to death, one each in Alabama, Arizona, Georgia, Mississippi, and Texas. They had served 30, 25, 28, 19, and 10 years, respectively. The longest-serving was EJI client Anthony Ray Hinton, who was exonerated and released last April after three decades on Alabama's death row. More than two-thirds of the people exonerated in homicide cases in 2015 were minorities; half were African American."

A shocking 27 exonerations last year were based on false confessions, where a record 65 were in guilty-plea cases. "More than 80 percent of the false confessions were in homicide cases, mostly by defendants who were under 18 or mentally handicapped or both, the registry reports." According to one report, "By any reasonable accounting, there are tens of thousands of false convictions each year across the country, and many more that have accumulated over the decades."

The statistics are staggering. And yet, they often leave us untouched. They are numbers, disembodied concepts that are made somehow unreal by their size and distance to our lives. Despite having always been opposed to the death penalty, it was the same for me for many years— ideology. That changed in 2010 when I became friends with a young man on death row in Mississippi named Matt Puckett. I had been inspired to correspond with him for this very reason: to humanize an issue that is all too dehumanized by the breadth and scope of the problem. My friendship with Matt (which is detailed in the afterword of "The Last Verdict") changed me forever.

In the same way, I want to help others experience the human realities around the death penalty. To that end I decided to write "The Last Verdict", a novella that is both a compelling legal thriller and a moving call to justice, to put human faces and voices to the issue of capital punishment.

However, I also wanted to provide readers with access to real people and real stories. That is why I have put together this important supplement to the novella. In the following pages you will find:

- **An interview with Ray Krone.** Ray is a death penalty abolitionist and the 100th inmate to be exonerated from death row since the death sentence was reinstated in 1976. In this compelling interview, Ray gives us a powerful and personal look into how easily an innocent man was sent to death row and the cost it exacted on his life.
- **An Interview with Mary Sennett Sellers.** Mary is the mother of my friend, Matt Puckett, who was executed by the state of Mississippi on March 20th, 2012. With beautiful honesty and passion, Mary helps us see the brokenness of the system that so easily neglects the families of the accused, leaving more and more victims in the wake of the original crime.

I hope that what you read here will impact you as much as it has impacted me. Thank you for your interest in this project.

-James L. Ricci, March 2016

INTERVIEW WITH
RAY KRONE

Jamie Arpin-Ricci: It is not uncommon for public perception of a person that is in prison—especially death row—to be that they are guilty and deserve to be there. How did you handle this strong presumption of guilt? What was it like to have so many believe the worst about you?

Ray Krone: You are right, if you get arrested for a violent crime, your name and face appear in many media outlets right away. The public has been lead to believe what they read/see there. What a burden for the wrongfully accused to overcome. I was embarrassed, ashamed and disgusted with this coverage at first and it bother me intensely.

Eventually I realized there was nothing I could do about that. The more important thing was proving my innocence. That became my focus and thankfully those who knew me believed and supported me. That's who I was then focused on and to hell with those who were wrong! I couldn't allow the ignorant and hateful people to destroy the good people I knew in my life!

JAR: You were once asked by an interviewer why God left you in prison for ten years. You answered by saying, "Maybe it's about the next ten years." What did you mean by that? What does it mean to you now, 14 years after your release?

RK: I felt that something positive must come from those years in prison. I became an advocate and voice for abolition, justice system reform, and encouragement for those facing injustice. I want that same public that accepted the original news stories to be ashamed and embarrassed like me and my family were.

I want them to believe one particular fact: if it could happen to me it can happen to anyone! I believe I've had success and that makes me very proud now that I fought the status quo and have so many people thank me for it.

JAR: If you could help people understand one thing about death row and capital punishment, what would it be?

RK: I think the fact that our justice system has repeatedly sentenced innocent people to death should outrage them. In addition I think they should know that it is a failed policy and not the "ultimate punishment" that they yearn for. If you want them to truly suffer, sentence them to life without parole, where they have to wake up everyday in our oppressive prisons knowing you'll never be freed and you deserve this suffering. Executing them is just letting them out of punishment. I know, I was on the row when people were executed and none of them whined or cried about dying, kill me and do me a favor!

JAR: Deservedly, you received two settlements after your release. Yet so many exonerated prisoners receive little to no support or compensation. While no amount of money can turn back the clock, why are these kinds of reparations important?

RK: We talk about justice and fairness as a cornerstone of our justice system. Well, then clearly restitution for those innocents is in line with that policy and belief. The financial and emotional costs to the accused and their family is extreme and should undoubtably be addressed in a modern, truly democratic society. Health, vocational assistance, education and public stigmatization are all issues that the exonerated must face and they deserve assistance from the same public/government that prosecuted them.

JAR: What keeps you awake at nights now? What are the most important battles you see ahead? What excites and gives you hope?

RK: I am mostly positive about the changes I've witnessed but am still worried about the unchecked powers of self-serving prosecutors and corrupt/incompetent investigators who face no consequences for their bad acts that truly put the public they are sworn to protect at more risk!

JAR: Thank you, Ray.

INTERVIEW WITH MARY STENNETT SELLERS

Jamie Arpin-Ricci: Before Matt's arrest and sentence, did you believe in capital punishment?

Mary Stennett Sellers: Before Matt, I don't remember thinking about capital punishment in the sense that I was for or against it. It had not affected my family before, so I didn't think about it or voice an opinion one way or the other. I would see images of people being executed in movies and that did not bother me too much because they had been portrayed as guilty. I would read about someone being sentenced to death in the news and it never really registered. I thought about the victims and their families, but never once thought about the convicted person's family or the new victims the death sentence created. Now, I realize that was a serious flaw in my way of thinking. It shouldn't have had to touch my life before I was able to express empathy for families that were fighting to save someone they loved.

JAR: When a person is imprisoned – even more so when they

are put on death row – people view their families as somehow
responsible as well. Did you experience that? In what ways?

MSS: Yes, almost from the very beginning and even
before Matt was arrested, the treatment from law enforcement was accusatory—we must be trying to hide him or
we knew more about the crime than we said we did. We
had no experience with the criminal system, the courts,
the jails or the people that worked in these areas. The
family of the victim had a personal relationship within
law enforcement, which only served to make the matter
worse. I still believe to this day that there were many officers of the law and courts who were more than willing to
perjure themselves or to look the other way while
evidence was fabricated and lies were told to insure that
Matt was convicted and executed simply to save the son of
a law enforcement officer.

We knew Matt better than anybody but trying to
convince the law that Matt could not have committed
such a heinous act was not possible. I worried about my
other boys who were still at home because there had been
death threats made against our family. Someone shot
windows out of a vehicle that Matt had once driven and
there was an attempt to break into our house. We lived in
a different but neighboring county from the one where
the crime was committed, so the law enforcement that
would answer our calls was much more professional and
respectful to us than law enforcement agencies where
Matt was in jail.

When Matt was convicted and sentenced, we sold our
home and moved away. I could not sleep at night worrying
that the corrupt system would come for my other boys
too. Most people would not say anything to our faces, but
we certainly knew that they were talking behind our

backs. Yet, despite what others thought about us, we refused to feel sorry for ourselves. After all, Matt had suffered the most by being falsely accused and imprisoned.

In the world today, where anything and everything can be found online, and with the capability to make anonymous comments, many people can be terribly biased and cruel. I feel sorry for people who post comments that promote killing on any level or for any reason. It truly makes me sad that so many people do not care about others, either innocent or guilty.

JAR: *Was there every a time where you doubted Matt's innocence? Can you tell us why or why not?*

MSS: I knew from the very second that I heard about the murder that Matt could not have been involved in the crime, but at the same time, I had so little information to go on, that I was a mass of confusion and emotion. I never doubted Matt but at the same time. I did question the version of events that we were given by law enforcement. I wondered about the how, the why, and the who?

It was probably 6 weeks after Matt was arrested that I received a call from him asking for his Dad and I to talk to the lawyer and schedule a private visit because he had something he wanted to tell us. My heart dropped as I weighed all of the possibilities of what he might say. What would I do if Matt told us that he was guilty? We would be beyond broken hearted but we would still stand beside him as he faced the consequences. He was our son and we loved him.

So Matt's Dad and I met with him and the lawyer in a small room at the county jail and I was able to touch him for the first time since he was arrested. That is when Matt explained to us what had happened on the day of the murder. When my husband and I walked out of the jail that day, we felt that a thousand concrete blocks had been lifted from our shoulders. Most if not all of our questions about what happened were answered and only served to reinforce Matt's innocence.

So, no, I never doubted his innocence, I just needed it to be shored up sometimes. It's a human nature thing. I know that Matt was able to have hope during his long, horrible years in prison because he knew that his family and his true friends supported him and believed in him and his innocence. And he left this world knowing that we still did.

JAR: Why do you want to see the death penalty ended?

MSS: A civilized country—and that is what we are supposed to be— should NEVER be in the business of murder. I cannot begin to describe the horror of having my son murdered by the State of Mississippi and to not be able to stop it from happening. I watched as the hearts of my entire family were shattered. We were all victims, as sure as the family of the murdered girl was.

Except Matt's murder could have been stopped before it was too late. There are so many cases of innocent people being exonerated in the news, more than 155 from death row alone. I think about how I would have felt if Matt had been exonerated and come home. He can't do that now, even if we were able to prove his innocence, because you cannot bring someone back from the grave. I want this world to be a better place and there is no room for the death penalty or murder in that better world.

JAR: What would Matt want us to do to honor his memory? What would he not want?

MSS: One of the last things that Matt told me was to "make them care". He wanted his family and his friends to promote love and caring for others, no matter who they were. Matt knew that there were people on death row that were guilty. He also knew there were some with very real mental problems. He knew that for the safety of others that those people needed to be imprisoned or they would

harm again, but Matt never wanted for them to be murdered by the state.

Matt wanted us to forgive the people who put him where he was and he meant everybody. In the very last conversation that I had with my precious son—a mere hour before he was murdered—he told me that I had to forgive EVERYBODY that had been a part of putting him in this place. He meant the family of the victim who hated him because they believed he had killed their loved one; those people who perjured themselves to insure a conviction; the district attorney; the judge and all involved in his being found guilty and made to spend 17 years in prison. Most especially, he wanted us to forgive the man who had actually committed the murder and allowed Matt to be charged, convicted and murdered for his crime. He knew that would be the hardest part for me.

Matt would not want any of us to mourn his passing or to lose one minute of happiness crying for him. He did not want us to continue to prove his innocence. He felt it would be a waste of time and resources. He believed that the truth would reveal itself in time and there would be a day of final justice for the guilty party. All he cared about was us believing in him and his innocence.

To make Matt proud of me, to fight to end the death penalty and to make others care is the very best way to honor his memory. That's all he asked.

*JAR: **Thank you, Mary.***

AFTERWORD

In 2010 I picked up John Grisham's latest novel, "The Confession" (Doubleday), which features the story of a wrongfully convicted man facing the death penalty. When I chose the book, I knew that I would be challenged in my thinking (after all, I have Grisham to blame for several major life choices inspired by his books), but I could not be prepared for the impact it would have on my life.

As I read the last page, I knew I had to do more than I was doing to see the death penalty put to an end. While I have always been opposed to capital punishment on an ideological level, the story humanized the realities in a way that changed me. I put the book down, picked up my laptop and began to look for ways to make a difference. One thing I decided that night was that I would correspond with men on death row. That is how I met Matt.

One of the reasons I decided to correspond with Matt, a death row inmate in Mississippi, was because we were born within a few weeks of each other. Being the same age allowed me to identify with him in a way that was startling. In the end, we became fast friends, sharing a passion for justice, a deep love of spirituality and faith, and the belief that the power of restorative justice and forgiveness was the only hopeful direction for us all. He introduced me to his family and many of his friends, allowing me to join the groups advocating to see his death sentence commuted, as well as those of other men and women on death row. Of all those amazing people, however, it was Matt's mother, Mary, who impacted me the most. She has become so dear to our family that "friend" seems too weak a term. We love her deeply. We all worked hard together to see true justice done.

And yet, for all the hard work and advocacy we engaged in, at 6:18pm on March 20th, 2012, the state of Mississippi declared Matt to be dead, killed by the state-sanctioned injection of deadly chemicals into his body. As I watched the clock tick down the seconds, knowing that Matt's life was ending, tears began to stream down my face. It was then that I began to imagine what Mary would be feeling in that moment. As a new parent myself, the thought of losing my son at all, let alone in this horrific way, crushed me. And again, I knew that I had to do something, to do more, to play whatever part I could to see that the death penalty would be ended forever.

Before he was executed, Matt asked me to use my writing to help the cause- not just his cause, but the larger work of ending the death penalty. He was always as deeply concerned for others as he was for himself, perhaps even more so. And so I began to spend the next few years learning everything I could about capital punishment, both in the United States and abroad. While I had initially been inspired to write because of my relational and emotional response to the death penalty, the research soon demonstrated that the death penalty is not merely morally and ethically wrong, but that it doesn't work, damaging countless innocent lives, needlessly costing tax payers millions, and in no way deterring violence and crime.

It is fitting that because it was a novel that changed my life so significantly it would be a novel I would write to change the perspective of others. As important as they are, I did not feel that I could write another non-fiction title about these issues that would add anything, at least not yet. Others have done that already and far better than I could. It was my hope that this story would let you, the reader, see another facet to the realities of this issue, another perspective on why we need to question the continued use of the death penalty in America —anywhere.

While not an exhaustive list, I wanted to point you towards several organizations that can help you better understand the complex realities of the death penalty, why it doesn't work, and the better alternatives that are already at work in the world around us. I hope that you will not only commit to learning more through these and other sources but that you will decide to get actively involved in some way.

Witness to Innocence (WTI):

Witness to Innocence is the nation's only organization dedicated to empowering exonerated death row survivors to be the most powerful and effective voice in the struggle to end the death penalty in the United States. Through public speaking, testifying in state legislatures, media work, and active participation in America's cultural life, their members are helping to end the death penalty by educating the public about innocence and wrongful convictions. WTI also provides an essential network of peer support for the exonerated, most of whom received no compensation or access to reentry services when released from death row.

Witness to Innocence initially began its program operations in 2003 under the fiscal sponsorship of the Moratorium Campaign Education Fund, a project of Sister Helen Prejean, renowned anti-death penalty activist, author, and Nobel Prize nominee. They launched their first visible national organizing campaign in September 2005, when 25 exonerated death row survivors, family members, and allies came together near Atlanta, Georgia, for a three-day gathering of the exonerated community. Since the official launching in 2005, they have played an essential and unique role in the anti-death penalty movement by sharing their stories with millions of people around the country and around the world.

A portion of the profits from this book will be donated to Witness to Innocence to support them in their important work.

www.witnesstoinnocence.org

Equal Justice Initiative (EJI):

The Equal Justice Initiative is a private, nonprofit organization that provides legal representation to indigent defendants and prisoners who have been denied fair and just treatment in the legal system. They litigate on behalf of condemned prisoners, juvenile offenders, people wrongly convicted or charged with violent crimes, poor people denied effective representation, and others whose trials are marked by racial bias or prosecutorial misconduct. EJI works with communities that have been marginalized by poverty and discouraged by unequal treatment. They also prepare reports, newsletters, and manuals to assist advocates and policymakers in the critically important work of reforming the administration of criminal justice.

www.eji.org

Bryan Stevenson, the Executive Director of EJI, has written an astonishing book which has gone on to be New York Times bestseller called "Just Mercy: A Story of Justice & Redemption" (Spiegel & Grau). I cannot more highly recommend this book.

www.bryanstevenson.com

The World Coalition Against the Death Penalty:

The World Coalition Against the Death Penalty is an alliance of more than 150 NGOs, bar associations, local authorities and unions that was created in Rome in 2002. It was founded as a result of the commitment made by the signatories of the Final Declaration of the 1st World Congress Against the Death Penalty organized by the French NGO Together Against the Death Penalty (ECPM) in Strasbourg in June 2001.

The aim of the World Coalition is to strengthen the international dimension of the fight against the death penalty. Its ultimate objective is to obtain the universal abolition of the death penalty. To achieve its goal, the World Coalition advocates for a definitive end to death sentences and executions in those countries where the death penalty is in force. In some countries, it is seeking to obtain a reduction in the use of capital punishment as a first step towards abolition.

www.worldcoalition.org

These are just a few of the many amazing organizations and activists involved in the movement to end the death penalty. I hope that they will give you a glimpse into the complexities behind this issue, as well as the hope that something should and can be done to change things. I am confident that if you give the information genuine consideration, you will be as convinced as I am that we need to work hard together to see this change happen. In the end, even if you remain convinced that the death penalty is an acceptable form of punishment, I hope that what you learn will temper your perspective with compassion and great caution. For myself, I cannot accept capital punishment at all, in any form, for any reason.

Some people have asked me if my friendship with Matt and other men on death row biases me on this issue. Of course it does. How could it not? That bias, however, is no less real than the bias in support of the death penalty born out of ideological extremes and caricatures of the accused. And yet, when faced with the honest truths about capital punishment, I believe that working for its abolition is the only rational, logical and moral choice we have. Therefore, my personal connection to people involved is not a problem, but an additional and valid support for the cause. It is not until people personally experience the systematic injustices so often related to these cases that they truly begin to see the death penalty for what it is. I take great joy to live in a time where the abolition of the death penalty seems to be within our grasp as more states begin to reject it. I hope this book will play some small part in these changes. That is up to you.

—Jamie Arpin-Ricci, 2016

ABOUT THE AUTHOR

Jamie Arpin-Ricci has been corresponding with men on death row for several years, actively engaging in the work to see capital punishment put to an end globally. He has written several books, as well as contributing to magazines and online publications. Born in Minnesota, he now lives in the West End of Winnipeg, Canada with his wife and son and works for a Christian non-profit that champions issues of peace and justice.

www.jamiearpinricci.com

ALSO BY JAMIE ARPIN-RICCI

www.jamiearpinricci.com/books

SUBSCRIBE

For news, updates, and special deal on books by Jamie
Arpin-Ricci, be sure to subscribe at:
www.jamiearpinricci.com/subscribe

YOUR EMAIL WILL NEVER BE SOLD OR PUBLICLY RELEASED.

www.ingramcontent.com/pod-product-compliance
Lightning Source LLC
Chambersburg PA
CBHW070640130626
46555CB00006B/2639